Awaken, Aurora

THE ESSENTIAL WITCH CHRONICLES

SYDNEY BROWN

Awaken, Aurora

THE ESSENTIAL WITCH CHRONICLES BEGIN

by Sydney Brown

Published by TLM Publishing House

5905 Atlanta Highway, Alpharetta GA.
https://www.ttpublishinghouse.com
Copyright © 2023 TLM Publishing House

Let's Connect

If you've enjoyed this book, you'll love what else is ahead!

Start out at https://www.essentialwitchchronicles.com to become part of the magic with a Facebook community where you'll find updates on the series, behind-the-scenes tidbits, and beta reader access whenever a new book is in the works!

Free Group:

https://www.facebook.com/groups/essentialwitch

Contents

Is This My Life?

Here I am, standing on the precipice of a new chapter in my life. I'm Aurora Hawthorn, a recent graduate from a modest college in Nowhere, Missouri, thrust into the kaleidoscope of diversity, dreams, and skyscrapers in Everwood, Georgia.

My rock, my anchor, in all this glorious chaos, is Liam, my boyfriend. Liam is a beacon of positivity, forever shining a light on the path ahead. He's got this magical way of making the future sound like an adventure just waiting to unfold.

"Aurora, you're on the brink of something extraordinary," he tells me, eyes twinkling like stars as he speaks of the days to come. "Just keep your eyes open; your big break is just around the bend."

Our apartment is a refuge and a serenity amidst the city's relentless energy. Here, we share dreams and ambitions over steaming cups of herbal tea and hearty, home-cooked meals. In these tender moments, hope feels almost palpable, like it's floating in the air between us.

"Any good news on the job front today?" Liam asks, his voice tinged with both eagerness and empathy.

I consider the day's treasure hunt for employment opportunities, pausing before I answer. "Nothing concrete yet, but something tells me I'm getting closer."

Outside, Everwood thrums with life. Its streets are a living, breathing organism, pulsating with people from every walk of life, each carrying their own dreams like invisible backpacks.

The city exudes a magnetic pull, a promise whispering in the wind that assures me, "Your moment is coming. Just you wait."

Above my desk hangs a vision board adorned with images of thriving businesses, successful entrepreneurs, and impressive corporate offices. It's a visual testament to my unwavering determination to make my mark in the world of business.

Weeks melt into months, but my resolve remains unshaken. Rejection emails and interviews that don't quite align with my vision may test my patience, but they can't break my spirit. Each setback fuels the fire of determination burning within me.

Without Liam, I'd be out on the streets after graduation. I certainly wasn't one of the lucky grads with offers lined up and waiting for me. But, still, I know, I feel it deep in my spirit; it's out there.

Our apartment is a haven of order and organization. Every item has its place, just as every step in my career plan is carefully outlined. Evenings are our respite, a time to unwind. We watch documentaries celebrating entrepreneurial triumphs or share dreams of financial stability and adventures in distant lands.

Liam has been such a great friend. When we met our freshman year, we just hit it off. He claims he knew it was love at first sight, but truth be told, it took me a bit longer to realize how great we complement each other.

I sit at my computer, scouring the classifieds for any job at this point. I'm in that place where I'm over-qualified for some jobs, but without real-life experience on my resume, I'm underqualified for the positions that I ache for.

I know it's unrealistic to hope to drop right in as a general manager of a big box store and set the world on fire, but come on, there must be something where I can gain the right experience and still feed my desire to be creative and bring order to the chaos.

I look out the window of our thirteen-story apartment. The skyline at night is remarkable. I wonder where everyone else works and if they also struggled to find a job.

I realize that I'm just another aspiring young professional with dreams that feel closer and farther than the same city skyline that greets me each day.

Career-wise, my vision is crystal clear—I am searching for my first professional job, one that will launch my business career like a rocket. The countless hours spent polishing my resume and crafting cover letters all boil down to this moment.

Each day, I eagerly scour job listings, hoping to find that elusive posting that feels tailor-made for me.

"Hey, hon, you okay?" Liam asks in his ever-so-subtle Irish accent as he rests his arm across my shoulder and begins to massage my neck gently.

"Yeah, I'm good," I try to convince him, "Do I seem stressed or something?" I smirk as I exaggerate an eye roll, so he won't see how worried I actually am.

"I'd say just a wee bit, yeah," he delivers a peck on my forehead, "But I'll let you keep up the strong charade for the moment. Don't worry, babe, I got you. I can take care of you forever if you'd only agree to allow it," he grins and winks as he walks back to the couch, grabbing the remote.

Liam was one of those graduates who had multiple job offers dropped in his lap before graduation. Granted, he's absolutely brilliant and deserves every offer he receives, but it helps that he's as gorgeous as he is brilliant. Throw in the accent, and interviewers are fully under his spell. He's magical to talk to and has the personality to back it up.

I think I can see the two of us moving through this life hand in hand. He certainly seems to be in it for the long run and treats me like a queen. I just always envisioned chasing my own dreams, and until he showed up in my life, I believed I would be reaching my goals on my own.

We share so many of the same visions and priorities, though; it's like the stars aligned the day we met. He literally bumped into me at a STEM club meeting when we were picking up our volunteer t-shirts.

We seem to agree on almost everything, with the exception of fish. He prefers them on plates, and I prefer them in tanks. Otherwise, we are basically the same person in different bodies.

I know he's sincere when he says I can take my time and wait for the perfect job. Maybe there isn't a perfect job for me. What happens if another month passes or six months? How long until he stops treating me like a queen and starts seeing me as a leech?

With renewed determination, I trail my focus back to the open job listings. This time, I enter the word *retail but* leave off the word *management*. Dozens of fresh job listings appear.

I just need to get my foot in the door somewhere. I can climb the ladder quickly with my degree, I convince myself.

A Stranger at the Door

"Bloody hell, Rora, look at this," Liam squeals from the other end of the living room, like I am not sitting only eight feet away. I turn to see what has his attention, imagining a spider or other crawling type. We seem to agree that capturing critters that make their way inside the apartment is my job.

I've never been a typical girly type, so I like capturing our uninvited guests, looking them over to see how they operate, and then setting them free to the balcony.

It's not often that Liam alerts me of an uninvited guest who's already out on the balcony, though, so I stand and try to focus on what he sees.

Liam stands near the sliding door, peering down at something quizzically. His brogue tinged his voice as he said, "Aurora, seriously, now, come have a look at this."

As I reach his side, my gaze falls into the darkness upon the most unexpected sight. There, on the concrete floor of our urban sanctuary, sits a cat unlike any I'd ever seen.

His fur is as dark as the midnight sky, a sleek and velvety black that seems to absorb the moonlight.

But it's not his color that leaves me in awe; it's a shimmering, almost ethereal glow that defies explanation.

I blink, half-expecting the cat to vanish into thin air. Yet, he remains, his bright, intelligent eyes locking onto mine. There's wisdom in his gaze, a knowing that transcends the mundane. At this moment, I realize that this is no ordinary feline.

"What... what is he?" I stammer my voice barely a whisper.

Liam shrugs, equally mystified. "I've no idea, love. But he appeared out of thin air, right here on our balcony."

We exchange a bewildered glance, trying to make sense of the inexplicable. There were no open windows or a way for the cat to climb thirteen stories. He is an enigma, a riddle we can't begin to solve.

He remains calm and regal, like a visitor from another world. He seems to understand our words and unspoken questions as if he is more than just a cat.

"He must have fallen from an upper-level balcony," I announce as if speaking the obvious seemed necessary to convince myself.

I extend a cautious hand toward him, and he nuzzles it affectionately, a purr rumbling deep within him.

"He doesn't seem hurt. His poor owners must be frantic right now, assuming the worst," I cautiously scoop up this gentle ball of fur.

"We'll fix that quick, now, won't we?" Liam grins as he grabs his loafers and heads toward the door, "Come on, love, there's only two stories above us, meaning he must have come from one of four apartments. Let's not leave them worrying any longer."

I take another look at our visitor in my arms, sense the overwhelming calm he brings, and realize that a tiny bit of me wants to keep him here with us for the night. He came to us, after all. But Liam is right. His owners deserve to know he's safe.

I slip into my shoes by the door, and off we go on an adventure. We step into the elevator, and I look down at this shiny raven beauty looking back at me.

He is shockingly calm for being in a stranger's arms and moving into the closing elevator. I wonder if he's familiar with the elevator already. I glance up at Liam with a sheepish grin.

"Now, don't give me that look, love. You know he belongs to someone already. We can't just steal someone's family member, now can we?"

"No. No, of course not. I don't want to steal him, but maybe I'll visit him once we find out where he lives. He's just so... comforting. I can't explain it."

Door by door, we meet three of our four upstairs neighbors, and all three smile and pet our new friend but affirm they don't own him. The fourth neighbor doesn't answer the door, so safe to say he likely lives in 1510.

"I guess you just got lucky, love. How about we take him home for the night and bring him back around in the morning?" Liam decides.

"Oh, yes. Let's! I wonder if we have anything he can eat for the night. Oh, but no litterbox," I visualize the worst-case scenario. "Maybe we'll let him sleep in the bathroom on a nice fluffy towel in case he has an accident."

"Sounds brilliant, dear heart," Liam taps me on the nose as if I've just solved a major dilemma, "And you and your new friend can get to know one another a bit better while I prepare for tomorrow's meeting with a new client."

We enter the code to our automatic door lock, walk back into the apartment, and look around as if to ensure no other visitors made their way in from the balcony. I go to the kitchen to grab a small bowl to put water in and realize my arms are full of cat.

As if reading my mind, Liam is on my heels, opens the cabinet, and takes out a delicate bowl from his grandmother's China collection.

"Oh no, not your grandmother's China. We don't know how he'll behave," I protest.

"It's this or one of my big cereal bowls, and I'm not sure we want something that big to be tipped. Besides, I have a feeling our little guest will be a perfect gentleman. Or lady? Do we know how to tell what it is?"

Liam suddenly seems awkward as I expose the cat's belly region.

"I honestly don't know. I've never had a cat, but there's nothing where a dog's, um, *thing*, would be. Maybe it's a girl?"

"Right. All right then, little miss, here's your water. Please do be a lady and treat Grandma Lillith's bowl with some respect," Liam looks at the cat in my arms, smiles, and dots her nose just as he had mine in the elevator. He'll be a great dad one day.

The moment arrives, and our little guest and Liam both look at me expectantly. I'm not sure why letting her go is so hard, but I gently set her down, and we both watch to see what she does.

She sniffs at the water in the bowl, looks at us as if to say, "Is this all you have?" and walks away, with us closely following.

After a few minutes, she's settled on the couch and seems to be perfectly content. Liam excuses himself to go to the spare room where his computer is set up to prepare for his morning meeting, leaving me staring at our guest.

"Well, I'm not going to find a job while I'm staring at you," I say to my new friend and head back to my desk in the living room.

"Where was I?" I rest my hand on the mouse and start scrolling the jobs. "Server. Nope. Commission Sales. Nope. Grill cook. Come on, really? No. No. No."

At that moment, Kitty jumps up in my lap, scaring the bejeezus out of me, but promptly relaxes. "Well, just make yourself comfy, Miss Thang," I say jokingly, but I find myself petting her beneath her chin as she rubs into my caress.

I click on the next page of job listings, and there it is!

"Entry-level management," I read aloud to myself, "Key Holder position. Essential Oils Boutique. Base Salary plus commission. Come grow with us." I feel a smile crawl across my face. "This could have some potential, huh, Miss Kitty?" I smile down at my new friend in my lap.

I promptly hit the *Easy Apply* button before I allow my sometimes overly analytical mind to talk me out of it.

"Looks like you may have brought me some good luck!"

"Hey, Liam, I think I'm going to go ahead and lie down. When you come to bed, will you put the kitty in the bathroom?" I call down the hall to the spare room. I don't want to tell him about the job listing I found just yet. Seeing the disappointment in his face again is more than I can stand.

It's bad enough to think he's disappointed in me, but what I usually see in his eyes feels more like pity, and I just can't take much more of that. I roll to my side, and as I start to drift off to sleep, I feel the kitty hop up on the bed beside me and situate herself at my feet.

I almost hope the neighbor at 1510 doesn't want her anymore. Fat chance of that, I acknowledge. Who wouldn't want this sweetie?

Awaken, Aurora: The Essential Witch Chronicles Begin

Finding the Litterbox

The alarm's melody blares, pulling me from sleep. It's still pitch-black outside, making me question if my phone's clock is playing tricks on me—or if we've somehow been transported to the Arctic Circle, where the sun has a more "flexible" schedule.

I shuffle in bed, turning to look at Liam and squint to make out the numbers on his alarm clock. That's when I feel a soft, furry presence at my feet.

Ah, the sweet cuddle of our accidental feline guest nestled at the foot of the bed. I smile; Liam must have caved and let her stay. It's either that, or she's a ninja cat that can pick locks.

And then it hits me. If Ninja Cat has been roaming freely all night, there's probably a 'gift' waiting for us somewhere—a liquid one. Visions of Liam stepping into an unexpected puddle send me leaping out of bed faster than a cat on a hot tin roof.

In full-on detective mode, I scour the apartment, half-expecting to find a mini ocean—or at least a small pond. Nothing. Zip. Nada. It gets me wondering—how long does it take for cat pee to evaporate, anyway? Is this a science experiment I'm willing to conduct?

Why didn't I just stick to the original plan and lock her in the bathroom? It's not like we're against animals; we're just against the messes they make. It was a pact: no pets until we had a yard for pets to play in.

As I stand there contemplating the lifespan of hidden cat urine, I realize that maybe, just maybe, our little intruder is more civilized than we thought. Or maybe she's just got her own secret bathroom that she's not sharing.

"Hey, love," Liam murmurs, his voice dripping with a sleepy sensuality that could give Barry White a run for his money. He squints one eye open, taking stock of my morning detective escapade. "Did our little furball gift us a puddle?"

"Surprisingly, no. She's either potty-trained or holding it in for her grand finale," I reply. "Wanna come upstairs with me to return her to her domain? She's probably missing her litter throne by now. But if you're in a hurry, I can play the knight in shining armor solo."

He gets up, sporting that irresistible 'I just woke up but still look amazing' vibe. "Oh, I'm coming with you. We're not about to have a rom-com moment where you meet the handsome neighbor and forget about me," he grins, landing a playful smack on my rear as he strides past me to the bathroom.

As the bathroom door shuts, I call out, "I hit the boyfriend jackpot with you!"

From behind the door, his voice floats back, full of mock arrogance, "Oh, I'm fully aware. But let's not forget, you're the Powerball to my scratch-off ticket. So yeah, #Blessed!"

Just moments later, we're standing in front of Apartment 1510, its door adorned with a quirky 'Home Sweet Home' sign that has seen better days. I hit the buzzer, and my ears catch the sound of multiple locks being undone—deadbolts, chain locks, you name it. This lady's apartment is like Fort Knox!

Finally, the door swings open to reveal a woman with a silver mane, enveloped in a floral housecoat so vibrant it could double as a garden. Her eyes are magnified by thick, oversized glasses that make her look like a pleasantly surprised owl.

When she spots the ball of black fur in my arms, her face breaks into a grin so warm it could melt butter.

"Morning, Ma'am," Liam greets, his smile as infectious as a pop tune. "We're your downstairs neighbors from 1310, and it seems we've found something—or someone—that might belong to you."

Her eyebrows rise in curiosity, "Oh? What might that be?"

Liam gestures toward our feline stowaway. "Well, this little guy crash-landed on our balcony last night. After playing Sherlock with the rest of the

17

upstairs tenants, we figured he had to be yours. You were MIA last night, so we kept him. Believe me, he's as eager to get back to his litter box as we are to steer clear of any 'accidents.'"

Her eyes widen, and she chuckles, "Oh, dear! I'm afraid the only thing I'm hosting are dust bunnies and a crippling fear of commitment. I'm also terribly allergic to cats. They make me sneeze louder than a firework on the Fourth of July. So, he's not mine, but best of luck finding his home!"

As she says her goodbyes and closes the door, Liam and I exchange puzzled looks, still holding onto a cat who's starting to look like a permanent fixture in our lives. The mystery deepens.

"Okay, so what's the game plan here? Call building management and have them alert animal control?" Liam says, his voice tinged with a pragmatic tone that screams, 'Let's solve this like a Sudoku puzzle.'

My mouth opens, and before my brain can intervene, I blurt, "Or—and hear me out—we could just order a pet starter pack online, a litter box, some kibble, and keep her till we figure out her story?"

Liam bursts into laughter. "Ah, there it is! I was wondering when one of us would float the idea of becoming accidental pet parents."

I cringe, suddenly aware of my spontaneous idea. "Oh God, ignore me. I'm being ridiculous. I mean, I'm basically a human financial sinkhole at the moment, and here I am, adding a fur baby to your budget. I can be so selfish."

Liam cuts me off, wagging a finger. "Hold it right there, drama queen. I was about to say I was wondering which of us would suggest it first. Because let me tell you, when I saw her cuddled at your feet last night, my heart did a little salsa dance. I knew giving her up would be like parting with a limb. So, problem solved!"

His eyes sparkle with a mischievous glint. "I'll order the feline VIP package, and you, my love, can book her a spa day at the vet. Let's make sure she's as healthy as she is mysterious. And preferably not expecting a litter of mini-mysteries."

I beam, my heart doing a jig of its own. "Deal," I say, locking eyes with our soon-to-be newest family member. "Welcome to the madhouse, Sweetie."

A Turn of Luck

We're perched in the vet's sterile office, the atmosphere buzzing with the subtle scent of antiseptic and kibble. Miss Kitty is safely ensconced in my lap, surveying her new temporary domain with the royal detachment only a cat can muster. My mind is a swirl of what-ifs and to-dos; the last few days have been a whirlwind.

First, Liam absolutely crushed it during his meeting with the new client. The man's like a business savant, making him a shoo-in for that junior partner gig.

I can already picture him casually leaning against his new mahogany corner desk, the corporate world's next big thing. Liam has this way of seizing the universe by its lapels and giving it a good shake. He's magnetic, a force of nature.

Then there's me. My phone buzzed the same day we officially inducted Miss Kitty into our domestic circus.

"Is this Aurora? Aurora Hawthorne?" A disembodied voice inquired. There are no prizes for guessing; caller ID flashed Mystic Aromas.

"It is," I replied, doing my best impression of a confident professional, which is kind of like a penguin trying to impersonate a peacock.

"Excellent. I have your resume in front of me. It looks like you've applied for our third-key position as a sales associate and management trainee. In reviewing your resume, you seem well-qualified... possibly over-qualified," her voice trailed off.

"No, ma'am, I do have a degree, but I'm aware that my lack of real-world experience requires that I start in an entry-level position, and I'm willing to work my way up," I stopped myself from going any further. I was already dripping with the sound of desperation.

After a few seconds, "Very well, I would like to invite you to come for a visit and see if you might be a good fit for our team. Are you available next Tuesday? Say 10:00 am?" the voice asks.

"Yes, ma'am. I can be there. Absolutely," again with desperation. "Could you tell me the address, please?"

"Of course, we're at 111 77th Place. It's down the road from the aquarium. I'm afraid it's in an older part of town. You might feel like you're going in the wrong direction, but if you use a GPS, it will bring you right to our door. Ask for Ms. Maxwell."

"Thank you very mu–" I began to say but realized she had hung up already. "I'm not sure that feels like a very promising sign," I said to Liam when updating him on my day.

"Come on, Rora, you're a magnet for great things. Exhibit A: moi," he grinned, pointing at himself.

"That's a lot of positivity to live up to," I half-joked.

So here we are, waiting for the vet to come and unravel Miss Kitty's enigmatic past, both of us absorbed in our individual worlds of career uncertainty.

For the first time, it feels like we're on divergent tracks. I'm all nerves, tangled up in doubts, while Liam seems to ride a wave of certainties.

It's unnerving, this momentary divergence. And as much as I love our little feline addition, I can't help but wonder: Are Liam and I drifting in different directions, or is this just the natural ebb and flow of a relationship in the real world?

Liam squeezes my hand, pulling me out of my reverie. "You okay, Rora?"

I smile weakly, "Just preoccupied. You?"

"Same," he nods, "but whatever happens, we'll navigate it together. New jobs, new pets, new adventures."

I look down at Miss Kitty, who chooses this exact moment to unleash a purr that could rival a lawnmower. "Well," I chuckle, "at least one of us is completely sure of her place in this world."

Liam laughs, "You and me both, Kitty. You and me both."

And just like that, my worries seem a bit smaller, the room a bit warmer. Maybe we're not so different after all.

"Good morning– or is it afternoon, the frazzled but friendly woman says as she exchanges smiles with us, "and who might you be?" she asks Miss Kitty in a playful voice. I wonder if she truly loves her job or if she's a great actor. Doesn't matter; she has me sold.

We share the mysterious way Miss Kitty showed up on our balcony as the doctor starts feeling around for whatever vets feel around for.

"Miss Kitty, huh?" she smiles at me and giggles softly, "Let me see here..."

The vet, a cheerful woman with an infectious smile, seems delighted, glancing between us both, her eyes widening as if she has a secret to tell, "Ah, yes, let's see what we've got here," she says, lifting Kitty gently. "Ah-ha! A boy! Well, a neutered one, but a boy nonetheless."

Liam and I exchange surprised glances. "Well, that's one existential crisis averted," I quip, making the vet chuckle.

24

"Looks like he's been cared for at some point, though," she adds, examining he– his well-groomed fur and clear eyes. "This little guy's been loved before, that's for sure."

We thank her, shop the supplies side of the store to stock up on all the first-pet-together goodies, and head out. It seems like we're becoming a family, whether we are ready or not.

As we head back to the car, the kitty comfortably settles in his new carrier, and Liam breaks the silence. "So, the big question—what do we call him? The vet's paperwork just says 'Black Cat,' which sounds either like a superhero or a bad omen but doesn't really fit our mysterious friend here."

I ponder for a moment, looking at his sleek black fur. "How about 'Obsidian'? It's strong, mysterious, and well, it's the same color as he is."

Liam grins. "Obsidian it is. But can we call him Obi for short? Makes him sound like a Jedi, and you know how I feel about Star Wars."

Laughing, I nod. "Obi it is. May the Force be with him."

"And also with you," Liam retorts, making a mock sign of the cross, which earns him a playful nudge from me.

As we drive home, I feel like Obi, or "Master Jedi Obi," as Liam has already started calling him, is the missing piece to our puzzle. A puzzle that, while never incomplete, somehow feels more whole with him in it.

Obi seems more than just content with his new name; it's as if he acknowledges it with a sense of regal approval. The first time Liam calls out, "Obi! Dinner time!" our enigmatic feline doesn't just saunter over; he strides as if he's been knighted. Sir Obi of Everwood, perhaps?

"I swear he knows he's named after a Jedi," Liam jokes, waving a fake lightsaber made from a rolled-up magazine. Obi looks up, his eyes narrowing as if to say, "The Force is strong with this one."

But as we both settle into an evening of Netflix and cat cuddles, the mystery of Obi's past looms like an unsolved riddle. I find myself staring at him as he nestles into a ball on his new plush cushion, his eyes meeting mine for a brief moment. They seem to hold a universe of untold stories.

"I just can't wrap my head around it, Liam," I finally say, breaking the cozy silence. "Where did he come from? Cats don't just defy gravity and drop onto a thirteenth-floor balcony. It's not like he's got a jetpack hidden under all that fur."

Liam laughs. "Well, if he does, he's keeping it a secret along with his past life as a feline spy or a circus acrobat. But you know, maybe that's okay. Maybe not knowing adds a bit of intrigue to our lives."

As if on cue, Obi stretches and yawns, displaying an air of mystery and contentment all at once. It's as if he's telling us, "Don't worry about my past; just focus on the now."

And in that moment, I realize that's enough. With Obi, we don't just have a pet; we've gained a family member wrapped in sleek black fur—a cat who might not have fallen from the sky but has certainly descended right into our hearts.

Awaken, Aurora: The Essential Witch Chronicles Begin

The Interview

Today is the day. Not just any day, mind you, but THE day—the Grand Poohbah of days, the pinnacle of my post-grad life thus far—my first professional job interview.

I've prepped for this like a squirrel stashing away acorns for the winter. I'm so ready; my nerves are doing the cha-cha in my stomach.

The GPS guides me to Mystic Aromas, an oasis of aromatic wonder tucked away in the eclectic quilt of shops and cafes in old Everwood, Georgia. As I step onto the cobblestone sidewalk, I can't help but feel like I've just walked into a fairy tale—only, hopefully, there are no wicked witches here. Unless they're hiring?

The boutique's façade is like a scene from a period drama, complete with an antique wrought-iron sign that's been naturally weathered—or expertly distressed, who knows?

Ivy spirals around its frame like nature's own graffiti. The window sports a hand-painted mural of herbs and botanicals, like a siren call to plant lovers and, well, witches. I cross my fingers, hoping the inside isn't so fragrant that I end up in a sneezing fit.

The wooden door is so heavy it's like opening a portal to Narnia. As it creaks open, I'm instantly swallowed up by a veritable smorgasbord of scents. It's like walking into an olfactory opera, where every aroma is a diva vying for the spotlight. My eyes take a moment to adjust to the soft, golden light that seems to caress everything it touches, like the sun flirting with the Earth.

I feel my heartbeat pick up tempo as it conducts an orchestra of emotions inside me. Before me are rows of glass bottles filled with liquids shimmering like a dragon's hoard. I half-expect them to start levitating or glowing on command.

The labels are a mishmash of cryptic symbols and arcane scripts, like the Rosetta Stone of essential oils. Some I recognize, thanks to my late-night Google deep dives. Others might as well be ancient hieroglyphics. For all I know, they could say, "Drink me and become a unicorn."

A collection of dried herbs and flowers in fancy jars catch my eye. They're organized with such meticulous care; it's like a librarian and a botanist had a love child, and this was their life's work. I stifle a chuckle, wondering if these are actually components for some Hogwarts-level potions.

At the back, there's a wooden counter that looks like a yard sale at Gandalf's house. It's adorned with curiosities like a crystal ball that I swear is winking at me, feathers that must've been plucked from phoenixes or at least very glamorous chickens, and vials of... well, let's just call them "mysteries."

Behind a velvet curtain—which totally ups the drama factor, by the way—is an alcove filled with leather-bound books that scream "ancient wisdom" or "antique store find." Either way, I'm intrigued.

Caught in the labyrinthine allure of Mystic Aromas, my attention is so scattered that I nearly leap out of my shoes when I sense someone behind me. Spinning around, I'm face-to-face with Ms. Maxwell, the proprietor of this aromatic wonderland and potentially my future boss.

Her eyes seem almost otherworldly, as if they've been dredging the depths of ancient seas and are now sifting through the flotsam and jetsam of my inner thoughts—and my questionable late-night YouTube clicks.

"You must be the job applicant," she intones, her voice a melodic mix of authority and warmth. The quiet tension in the room doesn't break; if anything, her words seem to thicken the air, charging it with an even more palpable sense of the extraordinary.

"You've arrived at Mystic Aromas, where our oils might be our heart, but the impossible is our soul."

Her lips stretch into a smile that somehow seems both cryptic and comforting. She gestures for me to approach, her hand moving through the air as if stirring invisible energies.

"Come closer, my dear," she says, her voice imbued with a gravity that makes it feel like she's imparting some ancient secret. "You're precisely where you're meant to be; I've been awaiting your arrival."

My heart is pounding like a drum solo at a rock concert. Is it the interview jitters, or is it the magnetic pull of the unknown that this store—and Ms. Maxwell herself—exude?

I step forward, feeling like I'm crossing an invisible threshold. It's more than a job interview now; it feels like the first chapter of an epic saga, and I'm both thrilled and terrified to read on.

Ms. Maxwell leads me to a small table near the front of the store, where two chairs sit facing each other. The table is covered with a deep purple cloth embroidered with intricate symbols and patterns that seem to shimmer in the soft light.

We take our seats, and I can't help but fidget from nervous energy. My palms feel slightly clammy as I glance around the store once more, taking in the myriad of bottles and ingredients that surround us; this time, I'm scoping out an exit strategy.

"I must admit," Ms. Maxwell begins, her eyes twinkling with a mixture of warmth and mystery, "I don't often conduct interviews for positions at Mystic

Aromas. Our work here is unique, and it requires a special kind of individual."

I nod, trying to hide the eagerness that wells up within me. This could very well be the opportunity I have been searching for, even if I don't fully understand what it entails. I see so much potential for bringing this little store into the current century and bringing efficiency and automation.

Ms. Maxwell continues, her voice soothing, "First of all, my name is Miriam. I invite you to call me by my first name now that I see you are a friend, albeit a bit timid for now. You see, here at Mystic Aromas, we work with essential oils, but not in the traditional sense. Our oils hold a deeper power, one that goes beyond the realm of casual aromatherapy. They are imbued with ancient wisdom and magic."

As she speaks, Miriam reaches for a small vial on the table. It contains a clear liquid that seems to shimmer like liquid moonlight. She uncorks the vial, and a faint, ethereal fragrance fills the air.

"Meet Moonlit Serenity," she says, handing me the small bottle as if she is handing over a crown jewel. "It's our Valium, our Zen Garden, and our 'Do Not Disturb' sign, all in one. It has the power to calm restless souls and soothe troubled minds. But it also plays a role in some of our more... esoteric recipes."

I accept the vial, marveling at its delicate beauty. It feels like I'm holding a piece of the cosmos in my hands, a tiny fragment of something infinitely larger.

Miriam's gaze never wavers as she studies me. "Aurora," she says, "we are a family here at Mystic Aromas, bound by a shared connection to the mystical world. We seek individuals who are not only skilled but also open to the wonders of magic."

I nod, my heart pounding. I have always been a practical person, rooted in the tangible world of business and logic. But at this moment, I feel a shift within me, a curiosity and yearning for something beyond the ordinary.

Miriam leans closer, her eyes locking onto mine. "Are you open to the mysteries that lie beyond the veil of reality, Aurora? Are you ready to embrace the extraordinary?"

Her words hang in the air, and I know that this was the moment of decision. I can choose to cling to the safety of the known or step into the uncharted territory of magic and wonder.

With a deep breath, I look into Miriam's eyes and say, "Yes, I am ready." I am immediately struck, wondering if I have just sold my soul to the devil or accepted a job offer.

Her smile widens, and it holds a promise of adventures and revelations yet to come. "Welcome to Mystic Aromas, Aurora Hawthorn. Your journey into the world of magic has just begun."

Miriam's words wash over me like a gentle breeze, and I feel a sense of destiny realized in the moment. It is as if the universe has guided me to this peculiar little store, to her, and this profound opportunity.

Miriam and I spend the next hour discussing the intricacies of the boutique, the unique properties of various essential oils, and the role they play in the creation of Mystic Aromas' products.

She explains how their customers often seek more than just pleasant scents; they seek solutions to life's challenges, both mundane and magical.

I am eager to learn, soaking in every word as if it were a spell waiting to be cast. Miriam's knowledge seems boundless, and I find myself hanging on to her every syllable.

Eventually, the interview concludes, and we stand up from our chairs. Miriam extends her hand, and I shake it firmly, sealing the unspoken agreement between us.

"You'll start tomorrow," she says with a warm smile. "We'll begin your training, and you'll soon discover the wonders of the oils we work with."

With a sense of anticipation and a newfound yearning, I leave Mystic Aromas, carrying with me the vial of Moonlit Serenity and the promise of a "magical" journey.

I feel a bit torn about trying to convince people that something like fragrances can fix their problems, but everyone needs something to believe in. I'm not brainwashing them. They choose what to believe. I am just here to help them find which oil is believed to help their issue.

As I walk down the streets of Old Everwood, I notice the world around me with fresh eyes. The spooky has become quaint, the ordinary has become extraordinary, and the familiar has taken on an aura of enchantment.

I can't wait to get home to share the good news with Liam. I have a job!

Oops!

My kitchen is transformed into a cozy aromatic sanctuary—or maybe it's just the clutter of essential oil bottles that now adorn the countertops. The glass vials reflect the soft, golden light streaming from the overhead light fixture, throwing rainbow-like prisms onto the beige tile backsplash. I shouldn't have splurged this early, not when I'm on the brink of getting an employee discount from Mystic Aromas.

But patience has never been my virtue; I had to scratch the itch. Googling wasn't enough tonight, even on the eve of starting the new job, so when I recalled a friend who sold essential oils, I texted and ran by her place to grab some of her surplus inventory.

Liam is out tonight, drowning in the euphoria of his impending promotion to junior partner. The chatter about his new responsibilities has been incessant.

The man is now practically a corporate deity, expected to mingle with clients, inspire the team, and probably even walk on water. He's soaring, and I couldn't be happier for him, even if that means I'll see him less. Still, a part of me wonders how our schedules will align with this newfound whirlpool of commitments.

Standing here alone, my eyes dart between the array of oil bottles and my tablet propped up against the cookie jar. I feel like a confused alchemist. Is there an expiration date on peppermint oil? Should I worry about mixing lavender and lemon? My internal monologue spirals as I grapple with the self-imposed complexity of this new hobby.

"Okay, Aurora, time to dive in," I mutter to myself. The screen of my tablet glows with several open tabs, each promising to reveal the 'secrets' of essential oil blending.

My notebook is open, pen uncapped; I'm ready to jot down my elixir formulas like a diligent student jotting down lecture notes. My inner business major is having a field day—this is the kind of documentation that would make any professor proud.

Taking a deep breath, I unscrew the cap off the lavender oil. Its floral scent fills the air as I cautiously count the drops trickling into a small glass dish. "Three drops of lavender for calmness," I narrate softly, envisioning a tranquil field of purple blooms.

Next, I reach for the citrus. "Two drops for zest and energy," I continue, picturing a sun-drenched orchard—finally, a drop of cedarwood to ground the blend. I imagine walking through a forest, the earthy aroma enveloping me.

I stir the oils, the anticipation building. Will this be the magic formula that calms my nerves and emboldens my spirit?

I lean in for a sniff. The scent hits me, but not in the way I hoped. Instead of serenity and zest, I'm met with an aroma that can only be described as 'athletic gnome post-jog.' I scrunch my nose. "Okay, maybe less lavender next time," I chuckle, jotting down my observations. "Or maybe gnome essence is the next big thing?"

As I screw the cap back onto the failed blend, I feel invigorated by the process. I let out a cackle at the thought of what Liam would think at the site of my mad science fun.

Sure, Liam is out there conquering the corporate world, but here I am, conquering my own tiny universe, one drop at a time. And who knows? Maybe next time, I'll create a scent that smells less like a gnome's gym bag and more like the peaceful, empowering sanctuary I'm striving for.

Eager to shake off the "athletic gnome" debacle, I turn my attention to a new fragrant frontier. This time, I'm going all-in on florals—rose for love, jasmine for sensuality, and a sprinkle of ylang-ylang for that exotic twist.

I visualize myself as the Coco Chanel of essential oils, delicately crafting scents that would make even a queen's nose twitch in delight.

My hands are steadier now, confident even, as I unscrew the caps. "Two drops of rose oil for romance," I whisper, picturing a lush Victorian rose garden bathed in dawn light—next, jasmine. "One drop for allure," and I'm mentally transported to a balmy evening under a jasmine-laden trellis. Finally, "One drop of ylang-ylang for that mysterious oomph," and suddenly I'm in a tropical rainforest, the air thick with nature's perfume.

I give the oils a ceremonious stir, like a bartender mixing a cocktail of dreams. The aroma rises to meet me, and I lean in for the grand olfactory unveiling.

The scent smacks me square in the face. It's not just a floral bouquet; it's a full-on botanical assault, like being caught in a monsoon of rose petals and jasmine blooms while someone blasts ylang-ylang from a cannon. I pull back, eyes widened, half-expecting to find a flower crown materializing on my head.

Jotting down my thoughts, I can't help but chuckle. "Note to self: Next time, aim for 'subtle garden stroll,' not 'floral hurricane.'"

While I might not have nailed the delicate art of perfumery just yet, each drop brings me closer to finding my own aromatic masterpiece. And in the meantime, I'm having a bloomin' good time exploring!

Emboldened by my floral escapades, I figure it's time to push the olfactory envelope. I eye the bottles of patchouli and vetiver, their dark liquids promising an earthy complexity. "A bit of Bohemian ruggedness could be interesting," I think, convinced I'm about to birth a scent that screams 'sophisticated hipster.'

Patchouli first. As the dropper releases the essence into my mixing bowl, I envision incense wafting through a vintage record shop. "One for the soul," I say, a poetic tear almost forming in my eye.

Next, the vetiver's smoky, woody aroma should add a robust undercurrent, like sipping bourbon in a well-worn leather chair. "One for depth," I announce, feeling like a maestro before the crescendo.

As I stir the blend, there's a moment of hopeful anticipation, like a chemist awaiting a groundbreaking reaction. And then it hits me—the scent is not so much 'Brooklyn artisanal coffee shop' as it is 'basement frat house post-kegger.'

My eyes water, and I cough, recoiling from my Frankenstein's monster of a concoction. The air is thick with an aroma that could only be described as 'Eau de stale beer meets unwashed dreadlocks.'

Gasping for clean air, I bolt from the kitchen, my retreat as dramatic as if I'd just set off a stink bomb. I can almost hear the blend cackling malevolently behind me. A mental note is hastily scribbled in the notepad of my mind: 'Patchouli and vetiver are frenemies. Do not invite them to the same party unless you're hosting an eviction.'

So, yeah, that was a crash course in what not to mix. But hey, isn't that what madcap adventures in aroma are all about? On to the next aromatic roller coaster!

Rolling up my metaphorical sleeves, I approach the final frontier: the bottle of Moonlit Serenity, a gift from Miriam. I don't even know what's in it or how much it costs, but maybe if I only use a drop or two.

I hold the bottle delicately to my nose, inhaling its ethereal aroma. I close my eyes, and for a moment, I'm awash in moonbeams and Zen. But hey, I'm still riding the high of my aromatic adventures.

Its scent is intoxicating all by itself, but tonight isn't about diffusing a nice scent. Tonight, I'm in alchemy mode—one more blend before I clean up and get ready for my first day tomorrow.

Eyes twinkling with a mix of reverence and a dash of drama, I array my chosen essential oils like a maestro before a grand orchestra. There's lavender for peace of mind, citrus for a spark of vitality, cedarwood for a firm, earthy grounding, rose to infuse the air with a hint of romance, jasmine to add a flirtatious undertone, and ylang-ylang for that all-important cosmic equilibrium.

Taking a deep breath, I prepare for the grand finale—a drop of Moonlit Serenity. "For serenity and levitation—no, no, scratch that—for preparation!" I whisper-correct myself as if uttering a sacred mantra.

I chuckle. Levitation? Come on, Aurora, you're blending oils, not casting spells. It must be the aromatic fumes playing tricks on my brain. Note to self: next time, open a window.

Just as I'm about to give myself a mental pat on the back for being so adventurous, the universe pulls a fast one. The moment the last drop of Moonlit Serenity hits the bowl, a sound shatters the silence—like a bolt of lightning smacking a tin roof in the middle of a tempest. A wisp of smoke spirals up as if a tiny genie is ascending to freedom.

And then, all hell—or heaven?—breaks loose. Obi, our usually gravity-obeying feline, chooses this exact moment to leap onto the counter and then... freezes. Mid-air. Like a cat version of Neo dodging bullets in 'The Matrix,' paws splayed, belly exposed.

My eyes nearly pop out of their sockets, and my heart feels like it's on a race to the finish line.

"What in the Merlin's beard just happened?" I gasp, staring at Obi, who's suspended in the air like a furry, upside-down chandelier.

OMG, Obi! I go to reach for him to save him from a fall, but as our eyes catch each other, it's evident that he's not the least bit scared. In fact, he seems as cool as a cucumber. A flying cucumber, but a cucumber just the same.

After what feels like an eternity but was probably just a second or two, Obi lands—and nails the dismount on the counter. He gives me a look of supreme feline arrogance as if to say, "Well done, human. You've just aced Alchemy 101, Kitchen Counter Edition."

Wide-eyed, heart pounding like a techno remix, I'm stuck in a mental loop: My cat just floated. In my kitchen. Because of essential oils? Or was it—no way—magic?

"OMG, OMG, what just happened? Did I actually—nope, can't be. Must. Get. Fresh. Air!" I mumble to myself like a person who's just seen a UFO. Or a floating cat. Same difference. I dash to the sliding door, yank it open, and inhale deeply as if trying to vacuum-clean my brain.

Planting myself by the open balcony door, I sit there, bewildered. I peek cautiously at Obi. Is he traumatized? Is he—oh, who am I kidding? He's grooming himself like he just won 'America's Next Top Cat Model.'

With a sigh that's half relief and half utter bewilderment, I hoist myself off the floor. Obi, for his part, seems to have moved on from levitational gymnastics to self-care, licking his paws with a nonchalance that's borderline offensive. If cats could smirk, he'd be nailing it right now.

"Okay, clean-up time," I declare to no one but myself, channeling my inner Marie Kondo as if tidying can erase what just unfolded. I feverishly wipe down the counters, stash the oils back into a box as if they're now radioactive, and literally run from the room like it's a crime scene.

Grabbing Obi in a bear hug, I bolt into the bedroom and dive under the covers. Obi looks at me as if to say, "Really, human? After that display of feline acrobatics, you think a blanket fort is gonna cut it?"

But it's too late. I'm under the covers, Obi beside me, and we're in this together—whatever this is. As sleep overtakes me, I think that we've both just crossed a line into a new dimension of reality—or insanity.

Awaken, Aurora: The Essential Witch Chronicles Begin

Am I Doing This?

Blasting through the airwaves, Kelly Clarkson's voice wakes me up like a bolt of lightning. For a moment, I'm disoriented—this isn't my usual wake-up jam of acoustic Lumineers. Then it hits me. Holy moly, it's MY alarm. I haven't heard that sound in months, not since my college days of cramming and ramen noodles.

"Shoot, I've got to move!" Panic floods my veins. Where's Liam? His side of the bed is empty, sheets cool to the touch. His alarm—a gentle hum of folk music—is suspiciously silent. He must've slipped out earlier, probably diving headfirst into another workday. Bless him. He's a one-man machine. But today, I've got my own whirlwind to step into.

I dart into the shower, letting the steamy water clear my foggy thoughts. Flashes of last night's olfactory escapade hit me like a wrecking ball. My god, was I hallucinating? Or auditioning for 'Harry Potter and the Aromatic Apocalypse'? If the staff at Mystic Aromas is breathing this stuff all day, they must be on another plane of existence.

As the water cascades down, a torrent of possibilities swirls around me. I could really make a difference at the store—modernize it, make it safer, maybe even introduce an AI-powered diffuser or something. I'm snapped out of my entrepreneurial daydream by a jolting realization.

"Dang it, we didn't even discuss pay!" My heart sinks like a stone in a pond. Base salary plus commission could mean anything from pocket change to a small fortune. What if this whole adventure turns out to be a bus ticket to Brokeville? "Stupid, stupid, stupid," I chastise myself, "You've got 'gullible' tattooed on your forehead, don't you?"

I'm on the brink of calling the whole thing off. Who am I to think I can peddle essential oils? I'm not some zen yogi; I'm a logic-loving, science-adhering realist.

Towel-drying my hair, I reach for my phone to dial Miriam and gracefully bow out. And then, a facepalm moment: in my overzealous quest for efficiency, I had cleared my call history before saving the store's number.

"Okay, Aurora, deep breaths," I tell myself. "You'll go in person, feel out the vibe, and then decide if you're the next aromatic guru or just a girl who gets stoned on essential oils and hallucinates about seeing her cat levitate."

With that, I steel myself for whatever awaits— be it a career in essential oils or another entry in my ever-growing list of 'Well, That Happened' moments.

##

The bus ride to Mystic Aromas drags on like an eternity, each stoplight a glaring red omen warning me to turn back. And this cobblestone sidewalk?

It's practically an obstacle course designed to trip me up before I reach my ill-fated destination. Every step feels like I'm walking deeper into a horror movie. The only thing missing is the suspenseful music.

Why am I even doing this to myself? The deeper I dive into my mental pros and cons list, the more it starts to resemble a bad comedy sketch.

It's like my brain is a courtroom, and the jury of inner critics is having a field day. Every step adds another tally to the "cons" column: creepy ambiance, check; unknown salary, check; potential for hallucinations, triple check.

And the pros? Oh, the pros are laughable. One singular, lonely pro sitting in the corner: it's a job. A job's a job, right? Isn't that what they say? You need a job to get a job, and since my inbox is a barren wasteland devoid of interview offers, this Mystic Aromas gig is starting to look like a life raft in an ocean of unemployment.

But let's be real, the moment I feel the slightest inkling of a headache or see even a whiff of another hallucination, I'm ghosting this place so fast they'll think they hired an actual spirit. I'll be out of there quicker than a cat on a hot tin roof—or, you know, a cat floating in mid-air in my kitchen because that's a thing that happens now, apparently. Deep breath, Aurora. You've got this. Sort of.

Okay, let's talk about Ms. Miriam Maxwell for a second. The woman practically exudes an air of mystical vampire chic.

Seriously, she looks like she could've been an extra in a Tim Burton film. And what was that cryptic talk about a 'family'? Did I stumble into the set of "Interview with the Vampire"? Because I did not sign up to be the main course at a bloodsucker buffet.

Are her 'family' members nocturnal? Is Mystic Aromas a front for a vampire coven? Maybe that's why the park up the street is always in the news for "unexplained disappearances."

They're luring desperate job-seekers like me to serve as an all-you-can-eat buffet! I can see the headlines now: "Local Woman Missing: Last Seen Entering Aromatherapy Shop."

Oh God, my tombstone is practically carving itself: "Here lies Aurora Hawthorne, who, in a moment of job-seeking desperation, walked willingly into the most glaringly obvious trap ever laid."

I snap out of my spiraling thoughts and realize I've been watching my feet this entire time like they're about to reveal the meaning of life. Lo and behold, they've carried me across two streets and right to the door of Mystic Aromas. This threshold, adorned with its weirdly inviting sign, feels like the gateway to the underworld.

This is it, Aurora. The last door you'll ever walk through... alive. Cue the ominous music.

As I hear a knock on the window, my eyes dart around like a meerkat on high alert. Where's it coming from? Is this part of their grand bloodsucking scheme? Then I see him—a young man with a face so kind it almost short-circuits my paranoia. He waves with a smile that would disarm a SWAT team.

Relieved but still cautious, I reach for the door handle. But before my fingers even make contact, the door swings open like it's starring in a horror movie jump-scare. A little jolt runs through me, but I manage to keep my composure.

"Aurora! We're so excited to meet you!" booms a voice. I refocus my eyes and see a woman built like she could be the star player in an all-female football league. "Come on in, don't be shy!" she beckons.

Well, here it is, the point of no return. I'm about to walk into my own doom, complete with a smile plastered on my face. Cue the funeral march.

But instead of fulfilling my dark comedic fantasies of being the main course in a vampire coven feast, they usher me inside, lock the door (not creepy at all), and guide me toward the back room brimming with ancient-looking books.

There, amidst the aroma of musty pages and whatever essential oil concoction they've got diffusing, stands Miriam. She's engrossed in a book placed on an elegant podium, making her look like some sort of occult professor.

She lifts her gaze to meet mine, her eyes twinkling with a mix of wisdom and...is that mischief?

Miriam's gaze pierces me like an arrow through a bullseye, the corners of her mouth curling up into a sly, knowing grin. "So, what have you been up to?" she asks her voice a blend of accusation and maternal warmth. "I sense an awakening in you. You've been busy since our last meeting, haven't you?"

Her words send a chill down my spine, but then she softens, her eyes twinkling as if she's in on a cosmic joke. "Tell me, have you met your companion yet?"

"Do you mean Liam, my boyfriend?" I stammer, caught off guard and a bit bewildered. "How did you even know about him?"

She chuckles softly. "No, darling, not a boyfriend. Your companion. Have any small creatures recently crossed your path? Cats, perhaps, or owls?"

It's like someone dropped a puzzle box in my lap, and the pieces are falling into place at warp speed. Obi. The mysterious cat who practically crash-landed into our lives. Could he be... my companion? And this job—why did it appear only after Obi showed up? How

52

did I land it without even hashing out the nitty-gritty details?

And then, the mother of all epiphanies hits me. Did I make Obi float in mid-air? Is this my awakening?

Miriam seems to read the whirlwind of thoughts swirling in my mind.

"Take a seat, my dear. You're connecting the dots, and it can be overwhelming. I'll give you a moment to digest all of this," she says, turning toward an older lady who exudes kindness.

"Agnes, please fetch Aurora some water and perhaps a snack in case she starts feeling dizzy. We need to open the store soon." Then she looks at a young man—Ethan—with a sense of shared experience. "Ethan, could you open the window to let in some fresh air? I bet you recall what it's like to be in her shoes; your awakening was just last year."

"Thank you," I manage to utter, a sense of numbing disbelief washing over me. If this is what they call an "awakening," it feels more like I've spiraled down a rabbit hole into a wonderland where my wildest imaginings are suddenly the new normal.

So here I sit, mind racing, heart pounding, on the precipice of something inexplicable. Welcome to my awakening, I guess.

About the Author

Sydney Brown has spent over thirty-five years in the business world and later in the corporate world. She has learned what works and what doesn't when the goal is to get out of the stale, vanilla world of the generations before us.

She believes that each person has at least one successful business, one book, and one grand adventure in them, but most people don't know how to figure out their best fit, so they stay where they are.

She is a best-selling author, speaker, and coach, helping people reach out of their current situation and reinvent themselves so they can do more than exist and survive while in this great space.

Personally, she's a mom of two adulting children and proudly owns the title of "Crazy Cat Lady" among her friends. After too many years of avoiding living life, she is on a mission to help others identify and begin their own "Great Ascension."

Let's Connect

If you've enjoyed this book, you'll love what else is ahead!

Start out at https://www.essentialwitchchronicles.com to become part of the magic with a Facebook community where you'll find updates on the series, behind-the-scenes tidbits, and beta reader access whenever a new book is in the works!

Free Groups:
https://www.facebook.com/groups/essentialwitch

Also From TLM Publishing House

FICTION –
Sydney Brown Presents Series
https://www.amazon.com/dp/B0BSBT36HN
The Mall Cadet Series
https://www.amazon.com/gp/product/B0B66MDK3T
All In or Nothing Series
https://www.amazon.com/dp/B0B7FW9W8M
The 7 Wishes Series
https://www.amazon.com/dp/B0B62XJY59
The Deception Series
https://www.amazon.com/dp/B0B5RNQMF1
The Forbidden Love Series (18+)
https://www.amazon.com/dp/B0B5SX24SX

NONFICTION –
How to Start It Series
https://www.amazon.com/dp/B09Y2QHDPM
Aromatherapy Alchemy
https://www.amazon.com/dp/B0CJ5DD5C1

www.ingramcontent.com/pod-product-compliance
Lightning Source LLC
Chambersburg PA
CBHW070649130626
46555CB00006B/2780